HOW RAVEN STOLE the SUN

HOW RAVEN STOLE the SUN

Story by Maria Williams
Illustrations by Felix Vigil

Tales of the People

National Museum of the American Indian

Smithsonian Institution

Washington, D.C., and New York

Abbeville Press Publishers

New York   London

A long time ago, Raven, or *Yeíl*, was pure white from the tips of his claws to the ends of his wings. He was very striking, like fresh snow in winter. This was so long ago that there were no stars, no moon, and no sun. People lived in total darkness, and their only light was from campfires. Raven was concerned about this.

The stars, moon, and sun were kept in large, beautifully carved boxes in a chief's house. The Chief was greedy and didn't want to share these wonders with anybody, not even his wife or daughter.

Raven knew the Chief kept the celestial lights all to himself and began plotting how he could take them away. Raven tried to get into the Chief's big house, but was always caught before he could enter. Finally, he came up with a brilliant scheme for stealing the stars, moon, and sun.

The Chief's daughter was a lovely young woman, and the Chief knew that soon she would be ready to have children of her own. This made him happy because he wanted grandchildren very badly, especially a grandson.

One day the daughter was gathering berries and got very thirsty. She found a nice creek flowing with fresh cool water. Raven quietly followed her, and as she began to scoop up water with her cup, he quickly transformed himself into a small pine needle. Raven drifted into her cup, and the young woman swallowed him.

Several months later the Chief's daughter gave birth to a beautiful baby boy. But what the Chief and his family didn't know was that the baby was Raven. The Chief was very happy and proud—he had always wanted a grandson! The baby cried a lot, but the Chief was very patient.

One day the Chief noticed the baby was pointing to the box with the stars in it. He cried and cried for it. Finally the Chief got the box of stars down to let his grandson play with it.

Raven smiled and played with the box, and when the Chief was not looking, Raven opened it. The stars flew out and up into the sky!

The grandfather was not pleased to lose his stars to the sky. But his grandson was happy for a little while, and this made him happy. But eventually Raven began to cry again. He cried and cried and pointed to the box containing the moon.

The Chief remembered what happened the last time, but couldn't stand to see his grandson cry, so he handed him the box with the moon in it.

The grandson smiled and played with the box. When the Chief looked away, Raven opened the lid. The moon flew out and up into the sky!

Raven loved making mischief, but he was growing tired of being a baby. He wanted to be a raven again. He missed his glorious feathers. He missed flying through the air, and he was getting really tired of the Chief. But Raven waited because he was so curious about what was in the last box, the biggest box, the most beautiful of the three boxes.

And so he began to cry. He cried and cried for days. The Chief remembered what had happened with the moon and the stars, but he was sad to see his grandson crying. So he handed him the last box, the box containing the sun.

Of course the cunning Raven was waiting for this moment. He opened the lid and freed the sun. What a beautiful sight! The sun flew out and up into the sky, and daylight came into the people's lives.

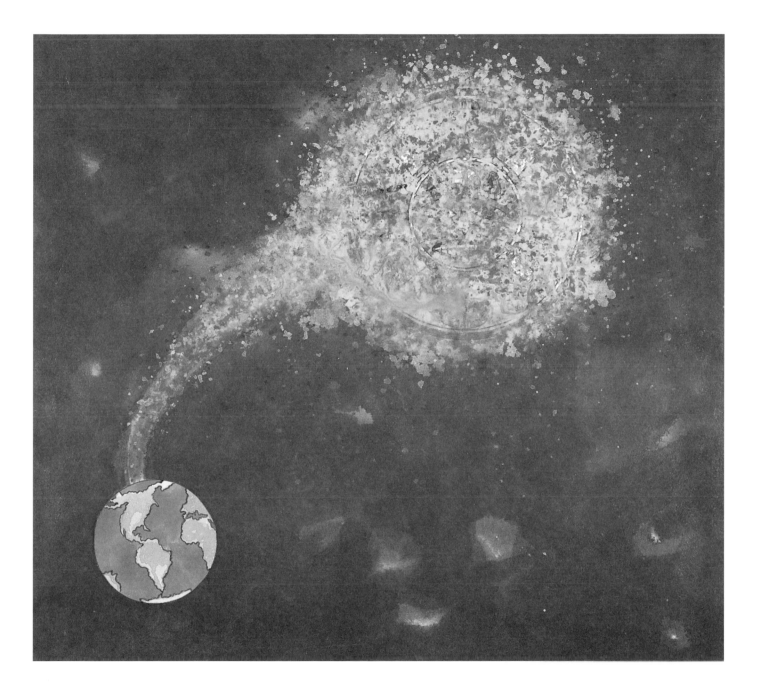

Raven was very happy, and now that his curiosity was satisfied
he changed back into a raven. The Chief saw the transformation
and became very angry. He had been tricked!

The Chief closed the door to the house and trapped Raven inside.
Raven knew the Chief was bigger and stronger and would
probably kill him. He flew around frantically trying to find
a way out.

Finally he spied a very small smokehole in the ceiling. He flew up to it and squeezed through, and as he did, the black soot coated his feathers. Raven joyfully burst out into the light of day.

Raven was very surprised to see that he was now completely black! From the tip of his claws to the ends of his wings, every feather and even his beak were a beautiful shiny black. This was how Raven came to be black, as he remains to this day.

Raven

Raven is a central figure throughout Northwest Coast historical legend. Accounts of Raven's deeds span the Pacific coast from Canada to Alaska. Raven stories are even found in Siberia. The tale of Raven stealing the sun is a traditional story throughout the region, yet each telling is a little different. Though the Tlingits say Raven became a pine needle in the cup of the Chief's daughter, the Athabaskans believe Raven turned into a small fish. In the Inuit version, Raven transforms into a piece of moss.

In Tlingit legendary history, Raven is both a compassionate creator and a mischief-maker. Raven not only stole the sun and ended darkness, but he also filled the oceans with land. According to tradition, Raven scattered sand from the bottom of the sea to the four corners of the world. Islands sprang up everywhere the grains of sand fell.

The great trickster was not always so helpful. For example, Raven created the first mosquitoes from a bag of crushed leaves. But despite Raven's mischief, the people of the Northwest know to respect his power. One chief learned the hard way when he killed Raven. The legend tells that all the lakes and rivers dried up, leaving nothing for his people to drink. After the chief put Raven back together the water returned, and now no one dares to kill a raven.

The handle of this Cape Fox Tlingit wooden potlatch spoon is carved to represent a raven. 14.9603.

Glossary of Tlingit Words

tribe	*kwan*
raven	*yeíl*
chief	*aankaáwoo*
mother	*tlaá*
father	*eésh*
daughter	*seé*
son	*yéet*
wife	*shat*
grandparent	*léelk'w*
grandchild	*dachxán*
box	*kóok*
child	*yádi* or *yádix*
sun	*gagáan*
sunlight	*a-d-gaan*
moon	*dís*
stars	*kadli.it'ji*
water	*héen*
black	*akaw*
white, snow	*dleit*

Yakutat Tlingit Chief in traditional dress. L440.

Chilkat Tlingit tunic with bear design.
Goat wool and cedar bark. 7076.

This wooden chest was made in the late 1700s or early 1800s by a Tsimshian carver. The Tsimshian, neighbors of the Tlingits, are known to be excellent woodworkers. The small faces on the lid are inlaid with shell, and the front panel of the chest is carved to represent the head of an undersea monster named Gonakadet, the guardian of wealth. 9.8027.

Tlingit People

Master woodworkers, weavers, and fishermen, the Tlingit (pronounced KLINK-it) people live on the coast and coastal islands of Alaska and northwest Canada. Tlingits, whose tribe name means "human beings," share a close link with the land and its creatures. The sea is a bountiful source of seaweed, shellfish, halibut, and other food. Cedar trees, bears, birds, goats, and salmon thrive along the rocky coastland. In this rough land of plenty, the Tlingit people respect the spirits surrounding them by using only what they need and returning to the land what they do not use.

The Tlingit tribe is made up of independent clans, each belonging to the Raven group or the Eagle group. These two groups marry each other and help each other with ceremonies. Each clan has its own crest, or symbol of the important spirits in the clan history. Some important crests are Raven, Sea Otter, Thunderbird, Killer Whale, and Beaver. By carving, painting, and weaving images of these powerful figures into ordinary objects such as tools and clothing, the Tlingit people reinforce their relationship with their founding ancestor-spirits.

One way the Tlingit people celebrate is through the potlatch memorial ceremony. The host invites another clan to join their tribe in the great feast, at which dancers from each clan dress up as halibuts, ravens, and other animals. Their costumes and gestures tell stories. Memorials last one to three days. Tribe members leave with a renewed sense of place in Tlingit society, and the host enjoys new prestige in the clan.

Button blankets are often worn at potlatches. This one was made by a member of the Tlingit Killer Whale Clan. 23.6180.

28

Clara Johnson Williams (*Sàtlèndui ù*, Taku River Tlingit), author Maria Williams's grandmother, carrying Maria's father, Bill Awèx, on her back. Atlin, British Columbia, Canada, ca. June 1922.

Tlingit Indians in traditional dance dress. Chilkat, Alaska. N36406. This photograph may have been taken at a potlatch. Look at the man in the center foreground—he is wearing the beaded bib pictured below.

Tlingit man in traditional dress, with bear dancer. L439.

Tlingit beaded bib with killer whale design. Alaska. 24.7455

Project Director and Head of Publications, NMAI: Terence Winch
Text, Photo, and Reseach Editor, NMAI: Amy Pickworth
Executive Editor, Abbeville: Christopher Lyon
Art Director, Abbeville: Julietta Cheung
Designer, Abbeville: Kate Brown, Ashley Benning
Production Editor, Abbeville: Ashley Benning
Production Manager, Abbeville: Louise Kurtz

For information about the National Museum of the American Indian, visit the NMAI Website at www.nmai.si.edu.

PHOTOGRAPHY CREDITS
Courtesy Marilyn Williams: p. 29 top left

First edition
10 9 8 7 6

Library of Congress Cataloging-in-Publication Data
Williams, Maria
How Raven stole the sun / story by Maria Williams; illustrations by Felix Vigil – 1st ed. p. cm. – (Tales of the people)
ISBN 978-0-7892-0163-8
1. Tlingit Indians—Folklore. 2. Tales–Alaska. [1. Tlingit Indians-Folklore. 2. Indians of North America-Alaska-Folklore. 3. Folklore-Alaska.] I. Vigil, Felix, ill. II. Title. III. Series.
E99. T6 W55 2001
398. 2′089′972–dc21   00-066348

For bulk and premium sales and for text adoption procedures, write to Customer Service Manager, Abbeville Press, 116 West 23rd Street, New York, NY 10011, or call 1-800-ARTBOOK.

Visit Abbeville Press online at www.abbeville.com.

The National Museum of the American Indian, Smithsonian Institution, is dedicated to working in collaboration with the indigenous peoples of the Americas to protect and foster Native cultures throughout the Western Hemisphere. The museum's publishing program seeks to augment awareness of Native American beliefs and lifeways, and to educate the public about the history and significance of Native cultures.

The museum's George Gustav Heye Center in Manhattan opened in 1994; its Cultural Resources Center opened in Suitland, Maryland, in 1998; in 2004, the museum celebrated the grand opening of its primary facility on the National Mall in Washington, D.C.

About the Author

Maria Williams (Tlingit) holds a Ph.D. in ethnomusicology from UCLA and was a contributor to the 1992 NMAI publication *Native American Dance: Ceremonies and Social Traditions*. An assistant research professor with the department of music at the University of New Mexico and the associate director for the Arts of the Americas Institute, Dr. Williams is currently a Ford Foundation postdoctoral research fellow, researching Native ceremonial dance and music with a focus on Alaska Native cultures.

About the Illustrator

As a child, Felix Vigil (Jicarilla Apache and Jemez Pueblo) spent many hours watching his father, Francis, paint. His father inspired him to pursue art as a professional career, and Felix went on to earn a B.F.A. in painting from the Maryland Institute College of Art in Baltimore. Mr. Vigil has been a professional artist for more than 25 years. He lives and paints in Jemez Pueblo, New Mexico, where he was born and raised. He exhibits his work regularly in galleries throughout the United States.

Tales of the People

Created with the Smithsonian's National Museum of the American Indian (NMAI), **Tales of the People** is a series of children's books celebrating Native American culture with illustrations and stories by Indian artists and writers. In addition to the tales themselves, each book also offers four pages filled with information and photographs exploring various aspects of Native culture, including a glossary of words in different Indian languages.